This book belongs to

....

ISBN 978-1-64638-670-3

www.cottagedoorpress.com

I Spy with My Little Eye

VALENTINE LOVE & FIND

Written by Rubie Crowe
Illustrated by Ella Bailey

cottage door press®

Did you know there's a special land where Valentines are sorted? Here, we birds train all year to make sure deliveries are perfectly transported.

Count 10 red envelopes.

Everyone is working hard and doing their best, but where is the bird that's taking a rest?

But when it comes to making deliveries to the toughest, wildest places, there's only one delivery bird who can do the job — she's clever, brave, and fearless.

Uh-oh! Can you find the truck with a flat tire?

Find 7 silly license plate

Do you see a pink envelope that fell out of someone's bag?

Dive down deep in the ocean blue
to deliver to fish, crustaceans, and whales?
I've got my flippers right here!
I'll deliver their Valentines without fail.

She wanted a ring
but she got a pearl.
Can you find
the lovesick girl?

I LUV U!

These yakety yaks are waiting for their Valentine's bouquets—they really love the stems. And I'll climb the tallest mountain to make sure they get them.

Do you see 6 yaks munching on tasty flower stem snacks?

There are so many ways to have fun in this mountain snow. Do you see a skier? A sledder? Look at them go!

The yaks have made a pretty mess with the flowers they tossed aside. I bet you could find 6 purple flowers if you really tried!

Count 7 snowy snow sculptures.

SNOW IN LOVE

The yaks aren't the only ones
who received Valentines today.
I spy with my little eye
4 wild geese flying by.

YOU'RE YAK-TASTIC!

A fight has broken out! But it's all in good fun.
The snowballs are flying. I wonder who won?

Delivering underground is a challenge,
but it's nothing I can't do!
Let me turn on my headlamp
and I'll tunnel my way through.

WOULD YOU GOPHER A VALENTINE DATE WITH ME?

YES

How do you help a cold naked mole rat?
Can you spy a Valentine sweater helping with that?

I spy with my little eye
a worm with a really nice perm.

Can you count 5 ants carrying Valentines?

Do you spy a cheesy present?

It's time for our bird to continue on her route.
Help her follow the ants to find her way out.

Bees are in the business of making honey and usually too busy for Valentine's Day. Not on my watch! Into their hive I go to deliver some special bouquets.

Can you spy a bee who got caught in a sticky situation?

The queen bee only likes Valentine gifts that begin with Can you find any bees who are bringing the right gifts?

BE BUDD

BEE MINE

Can you spy 4 members of the Bumble Bee Brass Band who have come to serenade the queen?

Do you spy a visiting fly?

Happy Valentine's Day.

U R SWEET

This bee accidentally flew away from their best bee buddy. Retrace their buzzy trail to help reunite them.

Count 5 blooming bouquets.

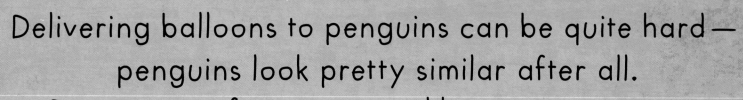

Delivering balloons to penguins can be quite hard—
penguins look pretty similar after all.
But it's easy for an expert like me to recognize
familiar faces and even some special penguin calls.

Count 5 balloons
in the shape of a heart.

Penguins use special calls to talk.
Can you find 3 penguins
with especially loud squawks?

This talented bird can shape
balloons however you wish.
Do you see a balloon flower,
a penguin, and a fish?

SNOW
CONES

Penguins are talented with ice, for sure.
Do you see 3 fancy ice sculptures?

I spy with my little eye
a milkshake made for two.

Two scoops are good,
but four are great!
Do you see a penguin sharing
is ice cream cone with their date?

Find a monkey missing all the fun because they're napping in the sun.

This artist's hearts are works of art. Do you see 7 hanging hearts in the trees?

High in the canopy are monkey families swinging haphazardly from the trees. But they can't get in my way—I deliver their boxes of chocolates with ease.

Can you find
7 butterflies
fluttering by?

Some monkeys don't
monkey around. Do you
see a monkey who is too
serious to celebrate?

Chocolates

Monkeys go bananas for
bananas. Can you count
10 yummy yellow treats?

The cacti and sand in the desert
make traveling tricky under the hot sun.
But armed with the right SPF and my visor,
delivering here is quite fun.

Count 3 cacti
in the shape of a heart.

HUG
ME

I'M WILD
ABOUT
YOU

A couple of jackrabbits named
Jack and Jill were having a great
Valentine's Day until ... they got separated.
Can you help them find each other?

It can be quite the difficult task to keep envelopes dry in a rainforest like this. But I'll be very careful, especially with the ones that are sealed with a kiss.

I am a potoo bird. My friends and I are shy. Do you spy 2 other potoo staring at you with their little yellow eyes?

Look at the frogs in so many hues. Count 8 but don't touch! They're poisonous to you.

The ants have something they want to discuss. Would you eat these treats instead of us? Count how many treats they have to share.

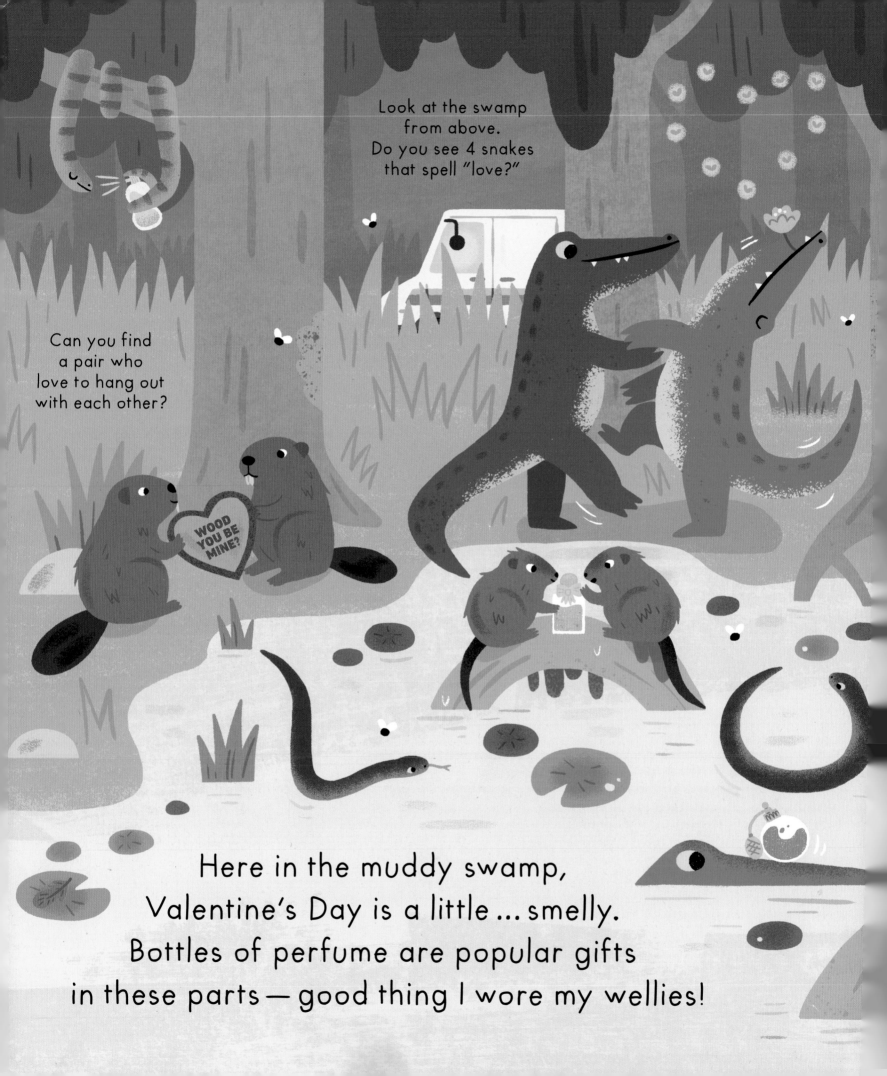

Look at the swamp
from above.
Do you see 4 snakes
that spell "love?"

Can you find
a pair who
love to hang out
with each other?

WOOD
YOU BE
MINE?

Here in the muddy swamp,
Valentine's Day is a little ... smelly.
Bottles of perfume are popular gifts
in these parts — good thing I wore my wellies!

Phew, everyone got their Valentine
in time—my day is complete!
Now I'm ready to go home
and rest my tired little bird feet.

YOU STOLE MY ♡

HOPPY VALENTINE'S DAY

Birds of a feather
flock together happily.
Who, hoo, do you spy
cuddling in their tree?

YOU ARE TOAD-ALLY AWESOME

HAVE A MICE DAY!

Find 2 matching purple flowers.